This Book Belongs To

For my son, Elan.

This book is dedicated in memory of my mother,
Charmayne Loercher and my sister Brenda.

Thank you to Eva Pfaff for her talent in
helping me put my vision on paper.

Special thanks to Elizabeth Auer for
prototyping the huggable Francisco!

Francisco The Ocean

Copyright © 2019, Anita Jo Loercher
Illustrations and cover by Eva Marie Pfaff
Follow Francisco the Littlest Goat on Facebook
www.franciscogoat.com

ISBN: 9781077419162

The Ocean

Francisco

THE LITTLEST GOAT WITH THE BIGGEST ADVENTURES!

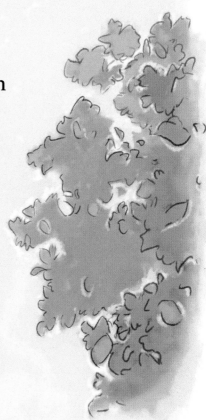

Every morning Francisco wakes up with
a positive attitude and a grateful heart.
As he ventures out to explore his world,
he loves to use his imagination!

Although he may be small in a
big world, he is brave.

8

This is Francisco! He may be small,
but he loves big adventures!

It was another beautiful, sunny morning!
Francisco was excited to begin his day!

1

Before Francisco started his journey, he paused
for a moment to enjoy the flowers.

They smelled wonderful!

It was a nice summer day! Francisco loved admiring all the different things that created his world!

Up ahead he noticed a path winding through some tall grass.

It looked very fun and inviting! Francisco wondered what he might find!

He stretched out his arms as he walked. The grass tickled!

The path suddenly came to an end. Francisco pulled the tall grass back to see what was on the other side.

Francisco had reached the ocean! The sun felt warm on his face.

He enjoyed watching the palm trees dance in the breeze!

Francisco loved shuffling his feet through the sand.

As the waves came ashore, he enjoyed splashing around!

He looked down and saw something in the sand. It was a cute little crab! "Well, Hello!" said Francisco. The crab scurried away.

Francisco looked up and noticed a little boat on the shore. "I think I will hop in and float for awhile." He was a little nervous, but reminded himself that he was very brave.

He used the oars to guide him as he drifted close to shore. Francisco liked the sound of the water as it splashed on the sides of the boat.

Francisco cautiously peeked over and saw something in the water. It swam around and around the boat!

It was a shark!
"My goodness!" exclaimed Francisco.

The shark gave a big, toothy smile to Francisco and swam away.

10

Francisco was amazed at how big the ocean was!

He sat back, closed his eyes, and took a deep breath. Francisco thought it was funny how his ears flapped in the wind!

12

Francisco rowed the boat back to shore.

As he stepped out of the boat, he saw a shadow on the sand. When he looked up, he saw lovely seagulls soaring gracefully in the sky.

Francisco sat down in the sand. The sunset was colorful
and the sound of the ocean was peaceful. It made his heart happy.

Francisco made his way back to the path to lead him home.

It was a lovely day!

Ok, maybe that ocean was just a pond and those palm trees were just mayapples.

Maybe the sand was just dirt.

Maybe that crab was just a snail.

16

Maybe that boat was just a lily pad and the oars were just cattails.

Maybe that shark was just a frog.

Maybe those seagulls were just dragonflies, but what a great adventure!

17

"No matter how small upon the earth,
Believe in yourself; give all that you're worth!"

～ Francisco ～

Francisco

"No matter how small upon the earth,
Believe in yourself; give all that you're worth!"

~ Francisco ~

Francisco Goat
P.O. Box 8035
East Peoria, IL 61611

PLACE
STAMP
HERE

Author, Anita Jo Loercher, also known as Nita Bita Luna, was born in Morton, Illinois. This is her second book in a series of Francisco stories. She has a love for children, art and nature. Her passion for these is portrayed through Francisco's confident character. He can see the big beautiful world around him and make it his own.

Illustrator, Eva Marie Pfaff grew up the oldest of 7 children, sketching away and having adventures in the woods of Illinois. She received an education at Illinois Central College and the Academy of Art University in San Francisco. She is also an Emmy Awarded Production Designer. Eva loves illustrating for stories that inspire make-believe and attempt to change the world.

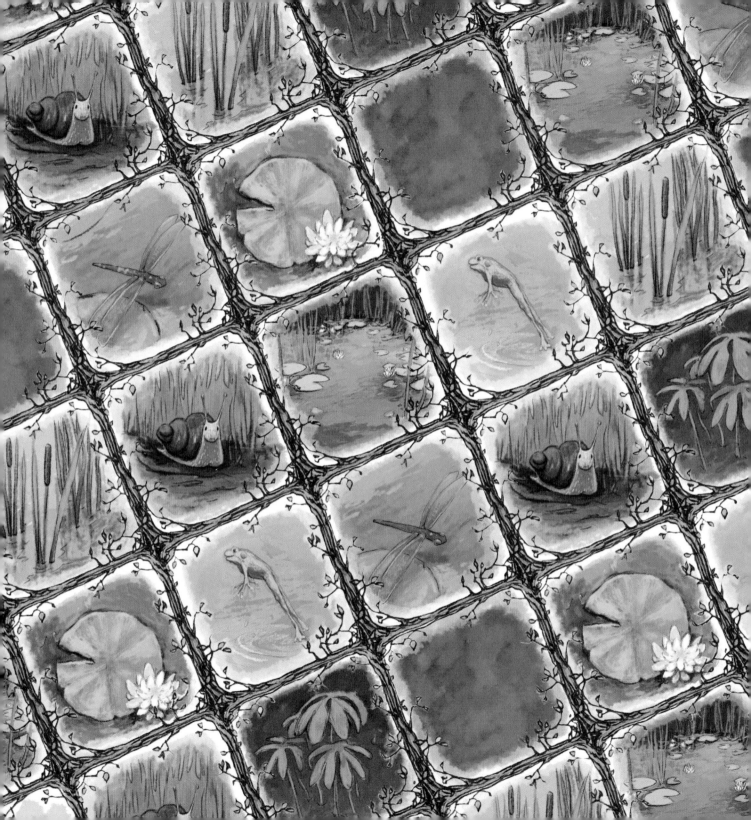

What did you discover on your adventure today?

Made in the USA
Las Vegas, NV
12 April 2021